Shopkins Shoppies

A PIECE OF CAKE

BY MEREDITH RUSU
ILLUSTRATIONS BY ARTFUL DOODLERS

SCHOLASTIC INC.

ISBN 978-1-338-13558-9

10 9 8 7 6 5 4 3 2 1   17 18 19 20 21

Printed in the U.S.A.   40

First printing 2017

Book design by Erin McMahon

Jessicake was at the Cupcake Queen Café trying a new recipe. But something was missing! She tasted the batter.

"Hmm," Jessicake said. "Cinnamon, chocolate chips . . . I know! Waffle crumbs!"

Jessicake picked up a bag and poured it into the bowl.

"Waffle crumbs?" asked Cherry Cake. "Will that taste good?"

"Trust me." Jessicake winked.

An hour later, Jessicake pulled a piping hot tray of cupcakes from the oven. She frosted them with graham cracker fudge icing.

"Chocolate Graham Waffle cupcakes, anyone?" she asked.

"Mmmm!" said Coco Cupcake. "These are just the sweetest!"

"It's no wonder customers are placing orders left and right for your cupcakes," said Cherry Cake.

The Berrylicious Gumdrop cupcakes Jessicake had made for Strawberry Kiss were a big success.

And everyone had buzzed about the Cookie-Crumble-Bumble cupcakes she made for Kooky Cookie's birthday party.

Jessicake had even whipped up some Dog Biscuit Delights and Catnip Caramel Crumbles for the Petkins. Everyone agreed: Jessicake's flavor combinations were the best in all of Shopville!

Suddenly, Shady Diva walked into the café.
"I need a special order, darling," she said.
"One thousand cupcakes by tomorrow night
for my fashion show. Follow this list of flavor
ideas exactly. Everything about this show
must be perfect!"

"One thousand cupcakes!" squeaked Jessicake. "I'm going to need some help!"

She called Popette and Bubbleisha.

"We're on our way!" said the Shoppies.

Popette and Bubbleisha hurried to the café. "Don't worry, Jessicake," exclaimed Popette. "Your baking buddies are here to save the day!"

"One thousand cupcakes *is* a tall order."
Bubblcisha snapped her gum. "I don't want to
burst your bubble, but can we pull it off?"
Jessicake smiled. "With the three of us
working together, it will be a piece of cake!"

The Shoppies put on their aprons and got ready to bake.

"Okay," said Jessicake. "Shady Diva asked us to follow this list exactly."

Just then, the front door bells jingled. It was
Apple Blossom and her dog, Milk Bud.

"Hi, Jessicake!" said Apple. "We're here to
pick up Milk Bud's Dog Biscuit Delights."

"Coming right up!" said Jessicake.

Milk Bud licked his lips at all the yummy smells floating through the bakery.

He sniffed the air . . .

He sniffed the counter . . .

He sniffed Shady Diva's list. It smelled like cupcake batter.

"Arf, arf!" Milk Bud snatched the list and ran off!

"Milk Bud, no!" cried Jessicake. "We need that list to make Shady Diva's cupcakes!"

Jessicake and Apple Blossom chased after him.

"I'll be right back!" Jessicake called over her shoulder to Popette and Bubbleisha.

Popette and Bubbleisha waited . . . and waited.

"If Jessicake doesn't get back soon, we'll never finish the cupcakes by tomorrow," Bubbleisha said.

Popette nodded. "You're right. It's time to get this show on the road!"

"But what about Shady Diva's list?" asked
Coco Cupcake. "Jessicake said we needed to
follow it exactly."

"Relax," said Popette, putting on a chef's
hat. "How hard can it be to whip up some
yummy cupcake flavors?"

So the Shoppies got cooking!

"A little butter . . . a little more butter . . ." Popette tasted her batter. "Hmmm. Needs more butter."

"And more popcorn!" added Bowl-inda and Polly Popcorn.

Bubblicious and Gumball Gabby helped
Bubbleisha stir a sugary masterpiece.

"Crushed candy!" cried Bubbleisha.

"More sprinkles!" shouted Bubblicious.

"Ooh—is that bubble gum frosting?" asked
Gumball Gabby.

Before long, the café was piled high with wild and crazy flavor creations!
There were Melted Butter Blast cupcakes . . .
Crushed Candy Confection cupcakes . . .

And even Perfect Popcorn Popover cupcakes.

Popette and Bubbleisha beamed. "They look PERFECT!"

Meanwhile, across Shopville, Jessicake and Apple Blossom chased Milk Bud.

"Milk Bud, please come back!" cried Jessicake. "Without that list, Shady Diva's special order will be a disaster!"

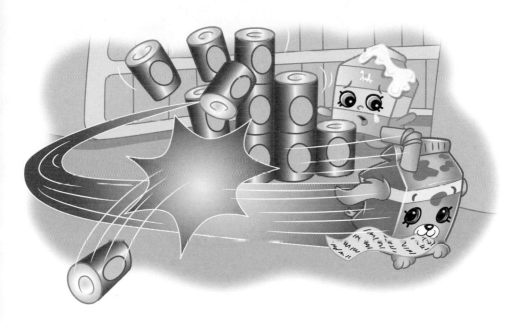

But Milk Bud would not stop. He zipped through Small Mart.

CRASH went the canned goods.

He zoomed through the park and dashed through the bushes.

And then . . . he sped toward the town fountain.

"No!" cried Jessicake.

SPLASH!

Shady Diva's flavor list was ruined.

"What do I do now?" Jessicake asked sadly.
"It's okay," said Apple. "I'm sure you can
think of flavors that will knock Shady Diva's
shades off, even without her special list."

Jessicake, Apple, and Milk Bud walked back to the Cupcake Queen Café. They arrived just in time to see Popette and Bubbleisha pulling the last batch of cupcakes out of the oven.

"What happened?" Jessicake asked.
"We baked one thousand cupcakes!" said Popette and Bubbleisha.

Jessicake shook her head. "Oh no. These aren't the cupcakes Shady Diva asked for! And now all the ingredients are gone. It's all . . . it's all . . ."

"Darlings!" a loud voice interrupted them. It was Shady Diva, back to check on the cupcakes.

The Shoppies held their breath as Shady
Diva picked up a Crushed Candy cupcake.
She took a bite. She chewed.
"What is this flavor?" she cried.

"Shady Diva, I can explain," started Jessicake.

But Shady Diva smiled. "This . . . this . . . is perfection!"

"It is?" asked Jessicake.

"I know I gave you a list to follow, darlings," said Shady Diva. "But these ingredients—butter, candy, popcorn! They are all perfect for my Classic Movies Fashion Show. However did you think up such perfect flavors?"

Jessicake grinned. "I had help," she admitted, "from two baking masters."

Popette and Bubbleisha nodded happily. "She sure did!"

The next night, the Shoppies enjoyed front
row seats at Shady Diva's fashion show.

"Thanks again for saving the day,"
Jessicake told her friends.

Bubbleisha grinned. "You were right. When
we worked together, it was a piece of cake!"